BOW-WOW
wiggle-waggle

Mary Newell DePalma

Eerdmans Books for Young Readers

Grand Rapids, Michigan • Cambridge, U.K.

Mary Newell DePalma has written and illustrated a number of children's books, including *Uh-Oh!* and *Now It Is Summer* (both Eerdmans), as well as *A Grand Old Tree* (Scholastic), which received the IRA/CBC Children's Choice award. Visit her website at www.marynewelldepalma.com.

Text and illustrations © 2012 Mary Newell DePalma

All rights reserved

Published in 2012 by
Eerdmans Books for Young Readers,
an imprint of Wm. B. Eerdmans Publishing Co.
2140 Oak Industrial Dr. NE
Grand Rapids, Michigan 49505
P.O. Box 163, Cambridge CB3 9PU U.K.

www.eerdmans.com/youngreaders

Manufactured at Tien Wah Press
in Singapore, February 2012, first printing

18 17 16 15 14 13 12   9 8 7 6 5 4 3 2 1

Library of Congress Cataloging-in-Publication Data

DePalma, Mary Newell.
Bow-wow wiggle-waggle / by Mary Newell DePalma;
illustrated by Mary Newell DePalma.
p. cm.
Summary: Simple, rhyming text follows a rambunctious
dog throughout a day of fun.
ISBN 978-0-8028-5408-7 (alk. paper)
[1. Stories in rhyme. 2. Dogs — Fiction.] I. Title.
PZ8.3.D437Bow 2012
[E] — dc23
2011035827

The illustrations were rendered in watercolor.

For Mary Margaret Newell
— *M.N.D.*

BOW-WOW

wiggle-
waggle

YIP-YAP

YOWL!

paw-paw

pitter-patter . . .

growL!

FLEE, FLY

FLUTTER-FLUTTER

FLICKER, FLASH

Honk! Honk!

puddle
paddle
waddle

GLIDE

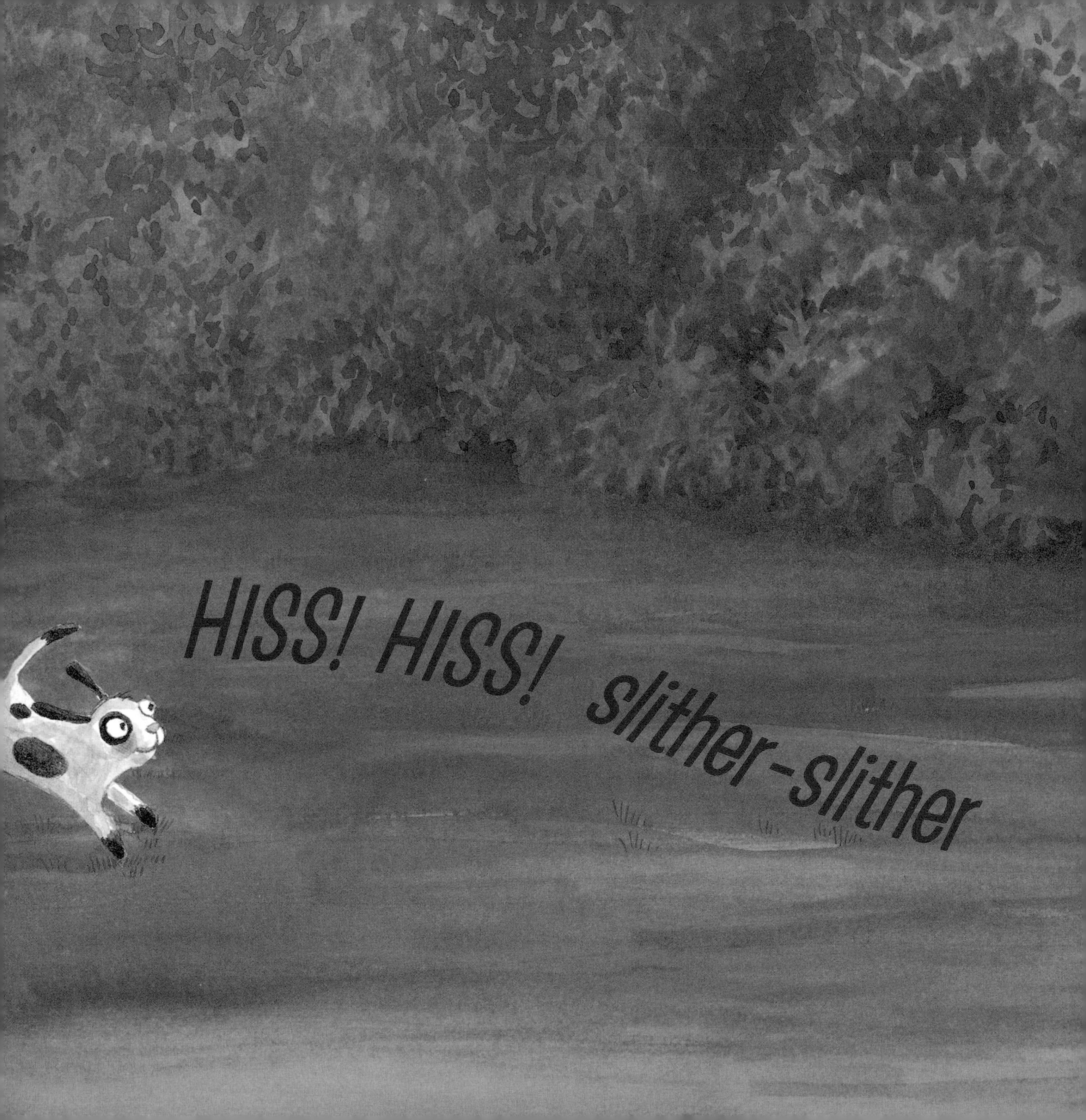
HISS! HISS! slither-slither

slip, slink, *slide*

TWITCH-TWITCH

shiver, quiver
nibble

BLINK

dart, dash

scatter

chatter

scamper

wink

BOW-WOW

wiggle-
waggle

sag, flag

sniffle-snuffle

sputter

bawl

swoop, loop
whistle, twitter

CALL crawl

scramble

ramble

zip, **skip** . . .

HUG, SNUG, TUMBLE, CUDDLE, PET, PAT . . .

pLay!